BREVELMEISTER AND KIRRINDER, STATIONERS

MORGENFELD

SEAN MONAGHAN

Published by Triple V Publishing

Cover illustration

© Grandfailure | Dreamstime

Paperback isbn: 978-1-0671081-5-1

Discover other titles by this author at:

www.seanmonaghan.com

BREVELMEISTER AND
KIRRINDER, STATIONERS

Chapter One

Turl ducked his head to pass under the rough oak beam right at the entry. The air was rich with the scents of ink and paper, and the walls in the narrow passage closed in on him. Turl just about had to turn sideways.

The sign above the door, decoratively chiseled into a slab of wood, had read *Brevelmaster and Kirrinder—Stationers*.

Turl was here to see Brevelmaster.

If he was still alive.

The walls were plaster and the passage was a good ten yards long. A strange way to lay out access to a stationery store. Any other place would have been facing out, with big windows displaying pens and pencils, bread erasers and trisquares and rulers, papers and notebooks and string and blades.

Turl ducked under another beam.

This building had to be two hundred years old. At least. Six or seven stories. Perhaps some basements to it as well. Old and settling. There were cracks in the walls and the wooden beams had aged to a deep gray smoothness.

It was cool. Turl was glad he'd thrown on a longcoat before he'd left. With his thick, comfortable leather boots, dark breeches, an undershirt, a patterned woolen shirt and a leather jerkin, he was dressed better than he usually might be. More formal, really. And the longcoat added to that. Almost like something a uniformed officer of the constabulary might wear on the way to an important arrest.

Remarkable how, just something like five blocks from his usual haunts, things could be so different. This was a darker, danker, denser part of the city. The corridors had little light and there were few courtyards or atriums. Among the hallways and passages of Morgenfeld, he was used to the soaring, high glass roofs and long plazas with sunlight making its way through intentional gaps in the structure. Places that brought the outside into the complex city byways and corridors that dominated.

From ahead came a soft clicking sound. Like when his cousin Eugenie drummed her fingernails on the edge of her drawing desk, waiting for him to pick up on some complicated idea she'd tossed out.

He loved her dearly, but she could be a little impatient. A little obtuse.

And here he was helping her out once again.

She would tell him that the narrow passage with the low beams was actually *regular* sized, and that he was just big. Mostly it didn't matter. Mostly places were built plenty large enough for people even bigger than he was. Not that there were many.

So what was up with this place? It was like a small, separate neighborhood where the architects and builders had decided that they wanted to discourage anyone who suffered from claustrophobia from coming anywhere near.

And why would that be? Was there something to hide?

At the end of the passage stood a wooden plank door, with a Z shape of structural boards on the near face. Held with fat black bolts and fingerleaf-shaped iron hinges.

Another odd thing. The door opened outward.

The door was just slightly ajar, and the clicking sound was coming from beyond.

Turl put his hand on the door's edge and pulled it toward himself. It opened into a dim room. Big. The walls felt distant. Shelving units and drawers stood around, not in rows. As if there had been an earthquake or someone barging around, knocking things out of alignment.

The smell was stronger, and now somewhat acrid and cloying. A kerosene lamp. Concentrated within the room. No natural light, and it felt like there was no ventilation, either.

"Brevelmaster?" Turl said. The room seemed to suck up his voice like a dishcloth sucked up water.

He took another step. The door creaked behind him, swinging back to its original position. The ceiling was higher than in the passage. Vaulted, with the arches just visible in the gloom.

Turl took another step. He rolled his shoulders. The room might be more spacious than the passage had been, but that didn't make it any more comfortable. Couldn't this Brevelmaster have had a store that was cozy and inviting? This place felt more abandoned, really.

There were plenty of abandoned parts of the city, that was for sure. To the south. Buildings rotting away, slowly turning back to the earth from which they'd risen.

This far north, though, this close to the Royal Palace and the new buildings going up at the city's northern edge, well, it was unusual.

The clicking continued. Turl inclined his head. Stepped around a cabinet. He got a glimpse of his own bare reflection in the glass front. Ghostly, almost vaporous in the dim light.

Inside, on the cabinet shelves, stood all manner of brass items. A fist-sized ball sitting on a ring. A cylindrical case housing a collection of brass circles that might have made some kind of compass or perhaps a calendar. A five-inch figurine of bear rearing on its hind legs.

Turl stepped on around. The clicking continued.

A heavy oak table stood in against the backs of more cabinets. Numerous clocks stood and lay on the table. Some were metal. Some were black with white hands and numbers, some were white with black features. One was a big cuckoo clock, with a peaked roof, the cuckoo itself bigger than Turl's thumb, stuck and leaning forward with the beak open as if the poor cuckoo was gasping its last. Next to it stood a foot-high glass dome with a complicated timepiece inside.

That was the source of the clicking. Ticking, really, since it was a clock.

A governor—was that the word?—kicked back and forth at the bottom, with dozens of tiny brass cogs in behind and above. The clock's face, the size of his palm, had three finely detailed hands pointing out from the center, and two other hands, smaller, off to the side. One had a circle of letters for the days of the week, M, T, W and so on, and the other had the numbers one through thirty-one.

Despite the operating governor and the clicking and the speeding second hand, the clock was wrong. Ten-fifteen on Thursday the twenty-first, when it was more like a little after nine on Tuesday the eighth.

"Ah," a voice said. "You're this man Turl about whom I've heard so much." Sultry. Feminine.

Turl turned.

A woman stood there, smiling at him. Tall enough that the top of her head came up above his shoulder height. She had petite nose and sparkling eyes and a scar like a burn mark smeared across her right cheek. Even with the scar, she was still attractive.

"You've heard so much about me?" he said.

"Taking down fifteen brigands with just your bare fists. Preventing the assassination of Archduke Milton Floister. Retrieving the stolen Demeter Stone and its gold setting. You're quite the hero."

"Rumors. Folk tales. Besides, I had help." They weren't rumors, but best if they were thought of that way.

"I understand," she said. "And here you are in my little store."

"You're Brevelmaster?"

"Katy," she said. "But not Brevelmaster. He's away. I'm Kirrinder. Katy Kirrinder. Charmed."

She held out her hand

Turl smiled. Took her hand and they shook. Her fingers were delicate, but the grip was firm.

"You knew I was coming?" he said.

"There was a message."

"Not from me."

"No. What the message didn't mention was why you were coming here."

"A few questions."

"An investigation?"

"Is he here?"

Katy licked her lips. Strangely sensual.

"You'd better come see." She picked up a lantern, turned and slipped away through the cabinets.

Turl followed. Through another narrow passageway, this one

with wood-paneled walls. Up an open spiral stairway with cast iron treads. The banister was cold against his hand. They went up at least two floors.

"It's an odd kind of store," Turl said. "Below."

"It hasn't been a going concern for some years now," Katy said. "My father used to tinker away and always had more work than he could manage."

"Stationers, though. I could smell it, but I didn't see much stationery. More clocks and such."

"The smell does linger, doesn't it. There are still stocks there, in some of the cabinets. " Katy's footfalls echoed around the stairway. Hard soles.

"What happened?"

"Brevelmaster happened. They'd been partners for three decades. Since before I was born. There was always a demand for stationery, bureaucracy being what it is around here."

"I know." Turl's cousin Eugenie was often mired in it with her work at the Map Archive.

Katy stepped from the top of the stairway into a wider corridor. Thick, patterned carpet on the floor. Doorways with wide, dark carved surrounds. A low, ceiling, decorated in the corner with webs, dusty and old.

The stairway had a central post reaching to the ceiling, and a balustrade around the hole.

Katy started along the corridor.

"What do you mean?" Turl said, "'Brevelmaster happened'? Explain that."

"I mean that Brevelmaster changed. A lot. Those clocks and other things, they were his idea. Branching out or something. There are plenty of fine clockmakers around the city, but he thought that the whole stationery thing wasn't bringing in enough money. He took over. Sidelined my father."

"Sidelined? How did he do that?"

"With a knife."

"A knife? He injured your father?"

Katy turned. "He killed my father."

Chapter Two

Along the high cornices of the corridor with the webs, there were regularly space light holes. Mirror tubes above, bringing daylight down through the building. A long-legged spider moved across one, lit up, colors on the abdomen showing.

Katy took a deep breath. She blinked. Turl imagined he could still hear the clicking from the store at the bottom of the spiral stairway. Had to be his imagination.

"Brevelmaster lost his mind?" Turl said. "Is that what you're saying. He was bringing clocks to the stationery store. He was sidelining your father. And Brevelmaster killed him. With a knife."

Katy blinked again, and looked away.

"The constabulary?" Turl said. "What did they do?"

"Nothing."

"Nothing? Are you saying that they don't know?"

"That's correct."

Turl's mouth felt dry. "Where is your father? His body."

"I don't know."

"So he could still be alive? Perhaps he just went on a trip." There were tours people could do these days. Guided walks through the Royal Palace or parts of the Tower of Bats. Boat trips on the enclosed rivers throughout the city.

"He didn't go on a trip. I saw it happen. I saw..." Katy trailed off. Took a breath. "I saw Brevelmaster plunge the knife into my father's belly. I saw my father collapse. That's not something you ever want to see. He raised me alone, you know that. I'm an orphan now. My mother passed when I was four. I barely remember her. And now... now he's gone too."

Katy was clearly holding herself together with a force of will.

Then something shifted in her. She stiffened. Stood more upright. She took a deep breath.

"I'm glad you're here. I don't have the strength for the next thing I need to do."

"What is that?"

"I'm showing you." Katy turned and started away along the corridor.

Turl followed.

"Are there other people in the building?" Turl said. There were so many places that were only half-occupied. Or less. But around here, this far north, there were usually plenty of people around.

"Just me," Katy said. "Just me and Brevelmaster. For the moment. And you, I suppose. You're here too."

"Residents, though?" The corridor certainly looked like a residential space. Homes behind those heavy doors.

"No one. Brevelmaster's brother and his family were here for a while a few years back. My father lived in a residence two floors up. I have a small place on the top floor. It makes for a lot of stairs to traverse to get to the store, but it is much lighter. Much more airy."

"I understand that." Even with the light tubes admitting sunlight, and Katy's lantern, it was still gloomy this far into the building. And the air was thick and slightly pungent. As if animals were colonizing the space. Something he'd come across plenty in places to the south. Nature taking over as the city decayed.

But something else too.

Tangy. Coppery.

Blood.

Turl prided himself on his senses. His ability to react a fraction of a second before an opponent did. His capacity to hear changes in the sounds of buildings—like the time that a small herd of horses had broken from a pen five buildings away from his own, and he'd known something was up, just from the change in the background sound.

But smell, that was something else. His friend Clara could distinguish easily between different kinds of herbs just from sniffing. But to Turl, the distinctions between cilantro and basil and sage were too subtle.

Katy led him through one of the doorways. Her lantern cast eerie shadows across the ragged walls. Old striped paper, peeling away, revealing the scrim below. Bare boards on the floor. A circular opening in the ceiling, reflecting light from high above. Dim, though. Something had maybe made a nest somewhere in the tube.

In the middle of the room, a man sat in a tall, angled chair. The kind of thing a barber might use to give a man a shave. Levers and iron pivots and struts. A shiny footrest.

The man was bound.

Thick ropes around his elbows held him to the arms of the

chair. His ankles were tied together, and into the part that held
the footrest in place. A cloth gag was tied tightly into his mouth,
pulling the corners back.

His eyes widened as he looked at Turl. Fear in them.

"What's happening here?" Turl said.

"You wanted to see Brevelmaster," Katy said. "This is him.
Thom Brevelmaster in all his limp glory."

"Why is he bound?"

Brevelmaster grunted.

"You know that," Katy said. "He killed my father."

Brevelmaster grunted some more.

"Eye for an eye," Katy said. "Tit for tat."

"Retribution?" Turl moved closer to Brevelmaster. "You need
to let the constabulary handle this."

There was a table in the corner, and on the table lay a blade.
A simple carving knife.

There were dark stains on the blade. Blood, perhaps.

"Constabulary?" Katy said. "You know what they will do?
Nothing. They will say there's not enough evidence. My word
against Brevelmaster's. And he's a respected member of the
community. At least, he *was*. With the mess he made of the
stationery business, there's less respect, I think. But still, it
carries weight. I'm just his business partner's daughter."

"You need to let him go. I'll take him to the constables. You
can come along. They'll lock him up. You can make your accusa-
tion. They'll note it all, and it will come before a magistrate."

"I'm not letting him go."

Turl sighed. Smiled to himself. There were legal gray areas all
over, that was for sure. Self-defense, reclaiming your property
when it had been stolen, trespassing in unclaimed parts of the
city.

There had been plenty of times when he himself had been

party to some of those. Theft and beating people because his friends were in mortal danger and he was the only one big enough and experienced enough to actually take on three assailants at once.

"You need to let the constabulary handle this," Turl said. Was this why Eugenie had sent him? Would she herself had just sided immediately with Katy, and Eugenie wanted to avoid that?

Katy frowned at him.

"I thought you could help," she said.

"I can. Let me take him to the constabulary. There's an office near here, isn't there?" His geography might be a bit off, but even if he took Brevelmaster back toward home, then he could just skirt on through to the Talbot office. A smaller one, but he knew some of the constables.

"That's not the kind of help I want," Katy said.

"It's the kind that I can offer." Turl went to Brevelmaster. Started to loosen the gag.

"Stop," Katy said. "Don't do that."

Turl stopped. Turned to look at her.

"You want my help," Turl said. "I'm giving it. You're bent out of shape because your father is dead. I understand that. But what you're doing here isn't going to help anything. Going through the right channels will. Constables, magistrate, and then your captive here is thrown in gaol."

"He won't be, though."

"So your solution is to tie him up here? You never needed me for this at all. If you'd have locked this room, the poor man would have starved to death long before anyone found him."

Katy glanced at the door.

"See," Turl said. "You want him taken care of, but you're not willing to step up and do the job yourself. What did you think by calling me here? That I would stick a blade into his gut when you're not brave enough to do so?"

Now Katy looked over toward the table.

"That wasn't an invitation," Turl said. "We're releasing him. I'll take him to face whatever he needs to face, but—"

"It wasn't him!" Katy yelped. She took a breath, then, quietly, said, "It wasn't him." The scar on her cheek had reddened.

"What do you mean?" Turl said

"It wasn't him that killed my father."

Brevelmaster grunted through the gag.

"So," Turl said. "He didn't kill your father. So what in the world is Brevelmaster doing here?"

"He would have, that's the point. He would have."

Turl shook his head. The woman was unhinged, clearly. To think that he'd thought she was attractive in that moment back in the store below.

"He would have?" Turl said. "Intent to commit a crime is not a crime. Unless there is evidence of preparation. He had preparation?"

"He made an attempt."

"An attempt. So, is your father still alive? Injured, perhaps."

"Oh, he's dead all right. No question. I buried him myself."

"You buried him?"

"Yes." Katy looked at the floor. Back up at Turl. Met his eyes.

"Please," Turl said, "tell me that you buried him through an undertaker."

She gave the tiniest shake of her head.

"Yourself?"

A nod.

"Where?"

It was hard burying people. Finding a space in the catacomb

crypts was time-consuming and difficult, and those old, tradi-tional burials with a dug grave in open ground were nigh unheard of. There were a few cemeteries around Morgenfeld, but most everyone went into the catacombs.

"Under the building," Katy whispered.

"This building?"

"I can show you? There's a basement and a sub basement. I can't stand upright. I wrapped him in muslin. Tarred it. Built a wooden box for him. Piled bricks and stones on top. Said a quiet prayer and sealed the access. We'd have to break open the door if I took you down."

Turl puffed out his cheeks. This woman was in a whole mess of trouble.

And not the kind of trouble from which he could extract her.

"Why did you do that?" Turl said.

"Scared. It was… it was almost as if I left my body. It wasn't me doing it. Someone else took over."

"Someone else?"

"A shadow self? Someone who knew what needed to be done and couldn't trust me myself to actually do it."

"Shadow self?" Turl was repeating her. He needed better questions. "Why did a shadow self take over?"

"Because it was me," Katy said. "Brevelmaster and my father were fighting. And Brevelmaster had the knife and he was trying to stab and cut him."

Brevelmaster grunted and squirmed in the chair.

"Keep going," Turl said, a sinking, weighty feeling settling over him.

"I burst in and tried to stop them. I joined the mêlée. I got the knife off Brevelmaster, but we were all so close and we stum-bled and fell and I landed on top of my father and I was still holding the knife and it went right into him and his eyes went so wide, staring into mine and then they just went blank. Went blank as the life fled him."

Chapter Three

In the room with the barber's chair and table with the knife and the peeling wallpaper, Turl looked at Brevelmaster. The man was wide-eyed. Terrified.

"You were holding the knife?" Turl said to Katy.

Her mouth formed a thin line.

Turl reached again for Brevelmaster's gag.

"Don't do that," Katy said. "Don't take that off."

"I'm sorry that it happened," Turl said. "It was an accident. Any magistrate would see that. You were stepping in to quell the fight and it went badly."

He kept working on the gag. It was tied tightly.

"But Brevelmaster could say the same thing," Katy said. "He could just say that I was estranged from my father. Resentful. That he found us fighting and stepped in himself and then we all tripped. And I was the one holding the blade."

"Were you estranged from your father?"

"No."

"So there's that. And I take it there was some history of antagonism between Brevelmaster and your father?"

"Absolutely."

"And that would be known?"

"Yes. I wish you would stop trying to take off the gag. Anything he might say will only cloud things."

"How so?"

"He'll deny it all. He'll say that my father was attacking him. Something like that."

Turl pulled the last of the knot holding the gag in place. It slipped away.

Brevelmaster gasped. Breathed out and in, like someone who'd just run up four flights of stairs.

"I—" he started, Turl cutting him off with a hand.

"Wait," Turl said.

"She's crazed," Brevelmaster said.

"I said wait. I would happily put this gag back in place."

Brevelmaster took another breath.

"You fought with her father?" Turl said. "Kirrinder?"

"We fought frequently. He believed the business could be run better. But he just meant differently. And we disagreed over how soon to pay our creditors. About how much overstock we should hold. About diversifying? You've seen our store below, haven't how?"

"I have," Turl said.

"Her." Brevelmaster nodded at Katy. "She brought all that upon us. Kirrinder said she knew what she was doing. Said he was training her to take over the business. Said we needed to have a succession plan."

Turl looked at Katy. She was shaking her head.

"See!" Brevelmaster said. "She's just—"

Again Turl held up his hand.

"Right now," Turl said, "I'm siding with her."

"She tied me up."

"And for now, that's how you're staying. But, Katy, I need to ask you some questions too."

Katy turned and left the room.

"You were supposed to help!" she shouted from outside.

"She's crazed," Brevelmaster said. "She needs the kind of help that only an institution can provide."

Turl knew of those kinds of places. Sad and overwhelmed. People shuffled out of sight so regular folks didn't have to see them.

"Stay here," Turl said, and followed Katy into the hallway.

She'd gone along, into the gloom at one of the other door-ways. She'd slumped to the floor, back against the door, knees up against her chest.

Turl walked along.

Crouched to her.

"Tell me," he said.

"Tell you what?" Her voice had gone quiet. Like a small child.

"How much of what he said in there was true. A succession plan. That you created the mess in the store." Jam-packed with cabinets.

"It's a temporary mess," Katy said. "This is what my father wanted. I know it."

"He told you?"

Katy didn't reply.

"This is not my specialty," Turl said. "Not this kind of thing. You need to get people from the constabulary here."

Katy shook her head.

"I have to let him go," Turl said. "I can't let you keep someone bound up."

Katy took a deep breath. She wiped her eyes.

"I understand," she said. "I'll come and help."

Chapter Four

Back in the room, Brevelmaster was struggling with his bonds. Succeeding only in giving himself welts on his wrists.

He didn't stop when they came in. He growled at them.

"We're going to let you go," Turl said. "But you've got to behave, all right?"

Brevelmaster nodded.

Turl went to Brevelmaster's left wrist and began working on the knot. The rope was as thick as Turl's little fingers, and finely woven. Katy had wound it around in tight loops. The knot felt as if it had been tugged into place with pliers. The fibers wouldn't budge.

"Watch out!" Brevelmaster said.

Turl stepped back.

Katy had retrieved the blade from the table.

Her eyes were narrowed.

"Put that down," Turl said.

"I'm just going to cut the ropes," Katy said. "Unless you want to spend all week untying them. I'm good with knots. They're tight, aren't they?"

"They are. Give me the knife then."

"What? You don't trust me with a blade?"

"What happened last time?" Turl said. "When your father and Brevelmaster were fighting?"

Katy licked her lips.

Barely audible, she said, "My father died."

"Yes," Turl said. "And who was holding the knife?"

"Me."

"Exactly."

"It was an accident." Katy took a step closer. "He was going to kill him. Kill my father. And he got what he wanted."

"I was never!" Brevelmaster said. "You need help Katy. Your father was too kind with you. Love blinded him. He couldn't—stop!"

Katy had jumped at him.

She slashed with the blade.

Chapter Five

Turl moved fast. Grabbed at her wrist.

Knocked it sideways.

The tip of the blade stabbed Brevelmaster's right upper arm.

He screamed.

Katy stepped back. She rocked. Knees bent, down on her hips. Arms wide, as if she was about wrap a child up in a hug.

Turl stepped around.

"He killed my father," Katy said.

"You killed him!" Brevelmaster screamed.

"You had the blade. You knocked me into him. You would have killed him anyway. If I hadn't come along."

Turl stood between them. The barber's chair rattled as Brevelmaster struggled.

"Give me the knife," Turl said. "This needs to go to the constabulary. You understand that, don't you?"

"They'll throw me in gaol."

"They should!" Brevelmaster shouted.

"Pipe down," Turl said. "You're only making things worse."

Katy's nostrils flared.

She stared into Turl's eyes.

"Make him admit it," Katy said.

"I'm bleeding here," Brevelmaster said.

"Knife," Turl said, holding out his hand. "Handle first."

"I'm not giving you the knife," Katy said. "You're on his side."

"I'm not on anyone's side. I just want you all to live long enough to get this resolved."

"How! How will it ever be resolved? Just make him admit it. Make him!"

"She's mad," Brevelmaster said. "Completely mad."

Katy darted forward. She ducked around Turl. Sprang at Brevelmaster.

Turl lunged. Caught her ankle as she rose.

Still, she swiped with the blade.

She caught Brevelmaster across the chest. Left a long, bloody slash.

Brevelmaster screamed again. The sound echoed around the room.

Katy landed across him. Right in his lap.

Turl kept hold of her ankle.

Brevelmaster bent his head. Bit at her.

She slapped him across the face.

Turl pulled her back. She was light. She flailed. Struggled.

Spun around. Slashed at him.

The blade sliced through the open flap of his longcoat.

He had both of her ankles. She'd fallen to the floor. On her back.

She jerked around.

Stabbed at him.

The tip of the blade went into his thigh. A scratch, but still something.

Something shifted for him right there. All the sympathy and concern vanished.

He yanked her around. Kicked her hand.

The blade went flying. Clattered against the floor.

Turl whipped her around. Got her upright. Pulled her elbows back. Put her wrists together. Held them in one hand.

"Ow, ow, ow!" she said. "That hurts."

"Little like my leg. Like Brevelmaster's arm and chest."

"He deserves it. My father is dead because of him."

Turl went to get the knife, hauling her along with him. She stumbled. Yelped.

Still holding her, Turl began cutting away Brevelmaster's bindings.

"Thank you," Brevelmaster said. He was breathing in gasps. His shirt was growing redder by the moment.

He lifted his freed arm and massaged his throat. The arm was bleeding too.

"We need to get you to an apothecary," Turl said. "Quickly."

"Bede is but a couple of buildings away."

"Good." Turl took the rope he'd unwound and used it to bind Katy's wrists. Satisfied she was secure, he let her go and worked quickly on freeing Brevelmaster.

"You shouldn't be doing that," Katy said. She was on her feet, arms bound behind her. Edging toward the door. "You know not of what he is capable."

"And you either," Turl said. "You lulled me, that's for sure."

"And he's lulled you."

"He's bleeding. We need to get him some help."

Turl cut the last of the ropes and Brevelmaster lurched to his feet. He was almost as big as Turl. How had Katy gotten Brevel-master bound into the seat?

Brevelmaster was breathing hard.

Katy had reached the doorway.

"You can walk all right?" Turl said to Brevelmaster. "We can go right to the apothecary."

Brevelmaster snorted.

He lurched again. This time, forward.

He ran at Katy.

She yelped. Sprinted away.

Chapter Six

Turl raced into the hallway after Brevelmaster. For someone bleeding so profusely, the man had a remarkable turn of speed.

When Turl reached the doorway, Katy was already halfway back along the hallway. Heading for the spiral stairway.

But her arms were bound. Her gait was messy.

Brevelmaster was moving faster.

"Stop!" Turl called.

Neither of them hesitated. They just kept running.

Turl hustled after them.

Katy reached the stairway just ahead of Brevelmaster.

She started down. Her shoes clattered against the steps.

Brevelmaster lunged for her. Stumbled. Fell to the carpet.

Katy yelped.

The clattering of her shoes was replaced with a series of thumps. And grunts. Bangs and cracks.

She yelped again.

Brevelmaster dragged himself along the floor. Tried to pull himself upright with the post at the top of the stairway.

He was on his knees when Turl reached him. Brevelmaster's shirt was red now. The blood was on the floor. Down through his pants. He leaned his head back and laughed.

"You hear that?" he said. "Hear that?"

There were no sounds from the stairway. Katy must have stopped tumbling.

"She fell!" Brevelmaster laughed some more. "Fell to her doom."

Brevelmaster was blocking the access to the stairway. His blood was down on the top steps.

He kept laughing. Maniacal.

Turl pulled him back.

"Stay here," Turl said.

Brevelmaster never stopped laughing. He was growing pale. Losing blood.

Turl hurried down. His fault. He'd bound her arms. Then she'd tried to run down the narrow, curving stairway. It would be difficult to keep her footing.

Turl kept his hand on the railing. Stepped on the wide outside of each tread as he descended.

Brevelmaster's laughter continued from above.

Turl went around a full circle. The light below was faint. Gloomy.

He found Katy at the bottom of the stairway. She lay on her back. Left leg up, foot on the second to bottom step. Her right leg was bent back at a nasty angle.

Turl stepped over. Crouched to her.

Her eyes were glazed and staring. There was blood on her forehead. In her hair.

Her nostrils flared.

Still breathing.

"Can you hear me?" Turl said.

"Uh," she said. Very quiet.

"Where does it hurt?"

"All... all over." Her breathing was shallow.

Brevelmaster laughed again. Something dripped from one of. the steps.

Blood? Brevelmaster's blood.

"I'm going to untie you," Turl said to Katy. He'd dropped the knife upstairs, but his knot wasn't anything like hers.

"Good," she said.

"So I'm going to tip you. On your side a little. So I can get to your wrists."

"Sure you are."

He took her right shoulder and hip and rolled her gently left.

"Oh, oh, ouch," she said.

"Just for a moment." Holding her hip, he prized open the knot. Let the rope fall away. Unwound it.

He pulled out her right arm and let her down again.

"Oh," she said. "Oops. That's better." She took a deep breath.

"Good. But you'll need to get up. We'll get you to some real help."

"What about him?" Katy's head flicked faintly. Indicating the top of the stairway.

Brevelmaster had stopped laughing.

"I'll come back for him," Turl said.

"Really? You're not going to take him first? He's hurt worse than me."

"Nah, it's not so bad. A scratch."

"You're not a good liar, Turl."

"But I practice so much."

She laughed. Then gasped. Eyes wide.

"Busted up your ribs maybe," Turl said. "Can you stand?"

She gave a shake of her head, puffing her breath in and out through pursed lips.

"I'll have to pick you up. It might hurt."

"Sure," Katy said, then she shouted, "Brevelmaster? Are you still alive?" She winced. Ribs.

There was no response. Another drip of blood fell through the stairway.

"All right," Katy said. "Carry me. Then you can get the constabulary and turn me in."

"I'm not going to turn you in. Bend your head forward." Turl crouched and slipped one arm across her shoulders and the other under her knees.

"You're not?"

"Nope. That would presumptuous." Turl lifted her. Katy sucked in air through clenched teeth.

"Presumptuous?" she said.

"I'll have to tell them about Brevelmaster, and you'll have to take them to your father. But I'm not turning you in. You can do that. See how things fall."

Turl adjusted his arms, trying to get the best grip. She was lighter than he'd expected.

"You're very kind," Katy said. "More than I expected."

"More than I expected too." Turl headed back through the store, negotiating his way between the cabinets. The place was a mess.

Perhaps this was what Eugenie had meant when she'd asked him to come down here.

Turl ducked his head to pass under the rough oak beams through the narrow passage that kind of closed in on him. He had to turn half-sideways with Katy in his arms. The scents of ink and paper hung in the air still.

"We could fix this place up," Turl said. "Turn it back into a going concern."

"A going concern? What do you mean?"

"Depending on what happens with Brevelmaster, I assume that the store will now be yours."

She gaped at him.

"I killed my father," she said. "And probably Brevelmaster. And you are talking about me just casually taking over the store?"

"An accident. Self-defense. And what else will you do?"

"Go to gaol. Or the gallows."

"I don't think so. You have me."

"You?"

"A witness. I saw how Brevelmaster changed when I released him."

Katy took a breath.

"But you saw how I was before that. With the knife."

She was right. She'd been half-crazed. Perhaps this wasn't such a great idea.

But then, among all of that, he liked her. The situation she'd been in had pushed something for her. She'd tied up Brevelmaster, and cut him.

Worse things had been excused.

They came to the wider corridor outside the store. Farther along, a man and a woman stood talking.

Turl looked at the carved sign above the door.

Brevelmaster and Kirrinder—Stationers.

Was that something he really wanted to delve into?

"Only one way," he whispered, "to know."

"What's that?" Katy said.

Turl smiled. Why was he so often attracted to women with a dangerous edge?

"Nothing," he said. "Just musing to myself. Come on, tell me the way to the apothecary so we can get you taken care of."

"And you'll come back?"

"I will. Not just for Brevelmaster."

"For me?"

Turl just smiled. His cousin Eugenie would definitely not approve.

But that was all right.

Afterword

When I wrote The Patrons of Art trilogy, set in the world of Morgenfeld, it was clear to me that Jason and Clara were the lead characters, but Turl was an important sidekick. He fills a role in those stories—*The Wintermas Paintings*, *The Bergeron Sculptures* and *The Ingersal Ballet*—that neither of them could.

Critical, to my mind, to the progression of the stories. But his role remains secondary.

Then, one day when I sat down at my writing computer, ready to start a new story, Turl showed up with a tale of his own. It was fun to hang out with him through the writing process, and I hope he was fun to hang out with for you as a reader.

There are more stories on the way. Some with characters from the original trilogies, and some with new characters, and part of my writing voice wonders if there will be novels with those new characters too.

It's hard to know where my writing voice will carry me.

I have such fun working in the world of Morgenfeld and there's so much history and so many lives to explore, and so very,

very many nooks and crannies, corridors and cupboards, attics and basements, and any number of open plazas and secret rooms, that some days I just about wonder if I could simply spend all my writing time just wandering around Morgenfeld telling those stories.

As always, there are many more ideas than I will ever have time to write.

Thanks for reading.

Sean
September 2025

About the Author

Award-winning author, Sean Monaghan has published more than one hundred stories in the U.S., the U.K., Australia, and in New Zealand, where he makes his home. A regular contributor to Asimov's, his story "Crimson Birds of Small Miracles", set in the art world of Shilinka Switalla, won both the Sir Julius Vogel Award, and the Asimov's Readers' Poll Award, for best short story.

He is a past winner of the Jim Baen Memorial Award, and the Amazing Stories Award.

Sean writes from a nook in a corner of his 110 year old home, usually listening to eighties music.

www.seanmonaghan.com

f facebook.com/seanmonaghanauthor
instagram.com/seanmonaghanauthor

Also by Sean Monaghan

MORGENFELD

MAP MAKER TRILOGY

The Mapmaker of Morgenfeld

The Stairs at Cronnenwood

The Chimneys in Atterton

PATRONS OF ART TRILOGY

The Wintermas Paintings

The Bergeron Sculptures

The Ingersal Ballet

MORGENFELD SHORT STORIES

The Quiet Hours

The Diorama

The Duchess, The Maid and the Ocelot

Bath Fish

Brevelmeister and Kirrinder, Stationers

OTHER FANTASY

Crossing Bonestrike Gorge

Sigrid's Eagle

KARNISH RIVER NAVIGATIONS

Arlchip Burnout

Canal Days

Eastern Foray

Guest House Izarra

Jackpot Kingdom

Liquid Machine

Night Operations

Persephone Quest

Rorqual Saitu

Tombs Under Vaile

Waxing Xebec

Yesterday's Ziggurat

CAPTAIN ARLON STODDARD ADVENTURES

Asteroid Jumpers

Ice Hunters

Ship Tracers

Core Runners

Desert Creepers

Underworld Climbers

Island hoppers

Mist Drifters

Dead Ringers

Tramp Steamers

Cradle Robbers

Margin Dwellers

CAPTAIN ARLON STODDARD Shorts

Ortanide Steppers (novella)

Sea Skimmers (short story)

Dark Behemoth (short story)

THE JUPITER FILES

Book 1: Deuterium Shine

Book 2: Tritium Blaze

STANDALONE SCIENCE FICTION

The Ergs

Raphael Marooned

Raven Rising

Athena Setting

The City Builders

The Cly

Gretel

SEAN
MONAGHAN
AUTHOR OF *THE MAP MAKER OF MORGENFELD*

MORGENFELD
THE WINTERMAS
PAINTINGS
A WHIMSICAL FANTASY NOVEL

The Wintermas Paintings
Book One
Morgenfeld—Patrons of Art Trilogy

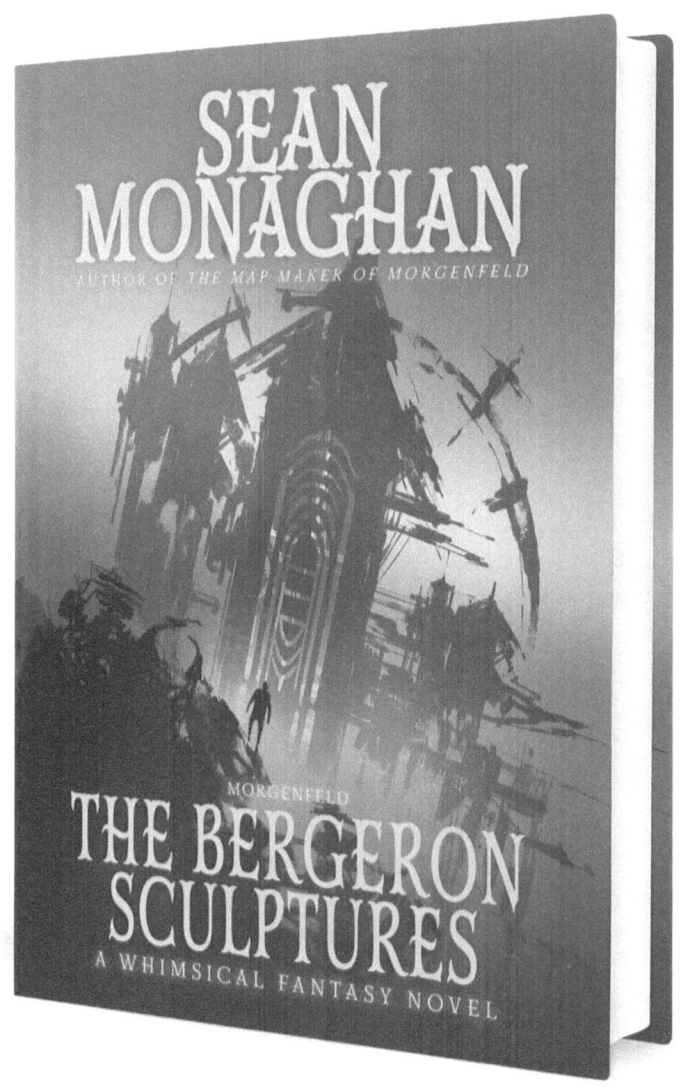

The Bergeron Sculptures

Book Two

Morgenfeld—Patrons of Art Trilogy

SEAN
MONAGHAN

AUTHOR OF *THE MAP MAKER OF MORGENFELD*

MORGENFELD
THE INGERSAL
BALLET
A WHIMSICAL FANTASY NOVEL

The Ingersal Ballet
Book Three
Morgenfeld—Patrons of Art Trilogy

www.ingramcontent.com/pod-product-compliance
Lightning Source LLC
Chambersburg PA
CBHW030240180626
46810CB00008B/3229